OF SPOTS

Lois Ehlert

P9-CIW-179

School of Fish

Spots and stripes,
when fish swim together,
tend to confuse
a hungry predator.

Skate

Flip, flop, swims the skate,
blending with ocean floor.
Digesting the shrimp it ate,
it hides and waits for more.

Eel

Like water bubbles,
its spots conceal
the devious movements
of an eel.

Flounder

A flounder is a flat fish,
a pancake with eyes topside.
It can change its colors
when it wants to hide.

Toad

When a toad
jumps in the air,
it shows off
spotted underwear.

Turtle

Turtle swimming—
spots are revealed.
Turtle sunning—
spots are concealed.

Chameleons

Chameleons can alter
the colors of their skin
to camouflage
the spot they're in.

Iguana

Why won't Mama let me get
this iguana for a pet?
"Its spots won't blend," she declares,
"with our couch and flowered chairs."

Rattlesnake

If a snake
shakes its rattle,
shake a leg—
and skedaddle!

Snake

When a snake's
high-strung,
it sticks out
its tongue.

Lizards

Lizards
slither
hither
and thither.

Goldfinch

When the weather's
warm and mellow,
a goldfinch turns
from dull to yellow.

Chickadee

Hearing a cheery
"chick-a-dee-dee"
identifies
the bird you see.

Oriole

Does an oriole
love oranges best
because the color
matches its breast?

Robin

Speckle-throated robin
chirps and cocks its head,
waiting for a worm
to crawl out of its bed.

Blue Jay

When a blue jay calls,
"Jay, jay, jay,"
the sound is the same
as its name.

Red-Winged Blackbird

Red and yellow patches
on each wing,
red-winged blackbird
sings of spring.

Hairy Woodpecker

How much wood
would a woodpecker wreck
if a woodpecker would peck
a wood deck?

Wood Duck

Striped head, eyes of red—
that's a wood duck male.
(Eyespots on head, instead?
That's a pale female.)

Loon

It's distinctive—
you can't mistake
loon's spots and stripes
out on a lake.

Red-Headed Woodpecker

If a woodpecker would peck
holes in a wood deck,
the whole deck, I suspect,
would be holey-wrecked.

Flicker

Rapid *tap-tap*—
that's a flicker sound,
tattooing on tree bark
where insects abound.

Spotted Owl

Unless there's a girl owl
and he's in pursuit,
a boy owl generally
won't give a hoot.

Goose

Migrating geese
fly in *V*s.
I wonder where
they catch some *Z*s?

Macaw

Gaudy macaw
is so conspicuous.
Trying to hide
would be ridiculous.

Toucan

Toucan's looking for a bird
of similar bill and feather,
so the two can live
happily together.

Barn Owl

One barn owl can catch
more mice and rats
than a whole family
of mouser cats.

Pheasant

Ring around the neck,
long striped tail:
pheasant strides and hides
on the brushy trail.

Roadrunner

The roadrunner is
a big cuckoo,
but in a road race
it might beat you.

Turkey

When a turkey
gobbles,
its warty wattle
wobbles.

Crowned Crane

Atop crane's head,
long neck beneath,
there is a crown:
a feathered wreath.

Humboldt Penguin

Orange streak
near its beak.
This penguin
is unique.

Frogs

Color spots warn:
These frogs taste icky.
Don't eat them
or you'll get sicky.

Panda

Same black eyespots,
same stripe near tummy.
Baby panda looks like
Dad and Mommy.

Badger

Masked badger,
a nighttime digger,
excavates burrows
with great vigor.

Goat

There's no dispute—
goat's face is cute.
But its horns can hit
right where you sit.

Anole Lizard

Lizard dressed up
and wants a date,
hoping to spot
a future mate.

Dalmatian

A dalmatian's
got lots
of splotchy
spots.

Cow

Spotted cow eats,
and by and by,
produces white milk
and brown cow pies.

White-Tailed Deer

Dappled spots
conceal newborn deer.
As the fawns grow,
their spots disappear.

Luna Moth

A moth's
flight
awaits
moonlight.

Buckeye Butterfly

Butterfly spots
look like big eyes
to scare the birds.
(It's a disguise!)

Cheetah

Running blur
of spotted fur—
you can't beat a
cheetah.

Tiger

Tiger stalks
with shiny eyes,
then takes its prey
by swift surprise.

Zebra Finch

A flying zebra?
It's a cinch—
if you are
a zebra finch.

Zebra

It must be hard to tell
when zebras join their friends
where one zebra starts
and another zebra ends.

Fritillary Butterfly

A nice thing
about a butterfly is that
it adds a spot of color
to our habitat.

Mandrill Baboon

Mandrill's face
is blue-striped and hairy.
Some find it attractive;
others find it scary.

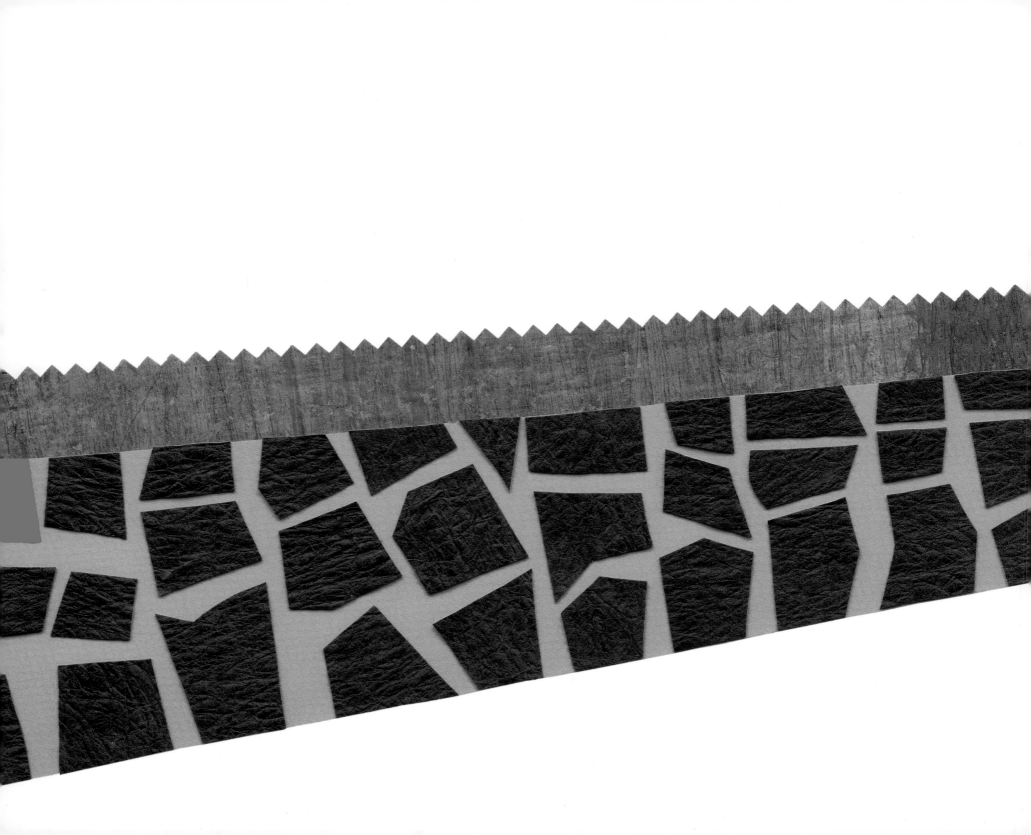

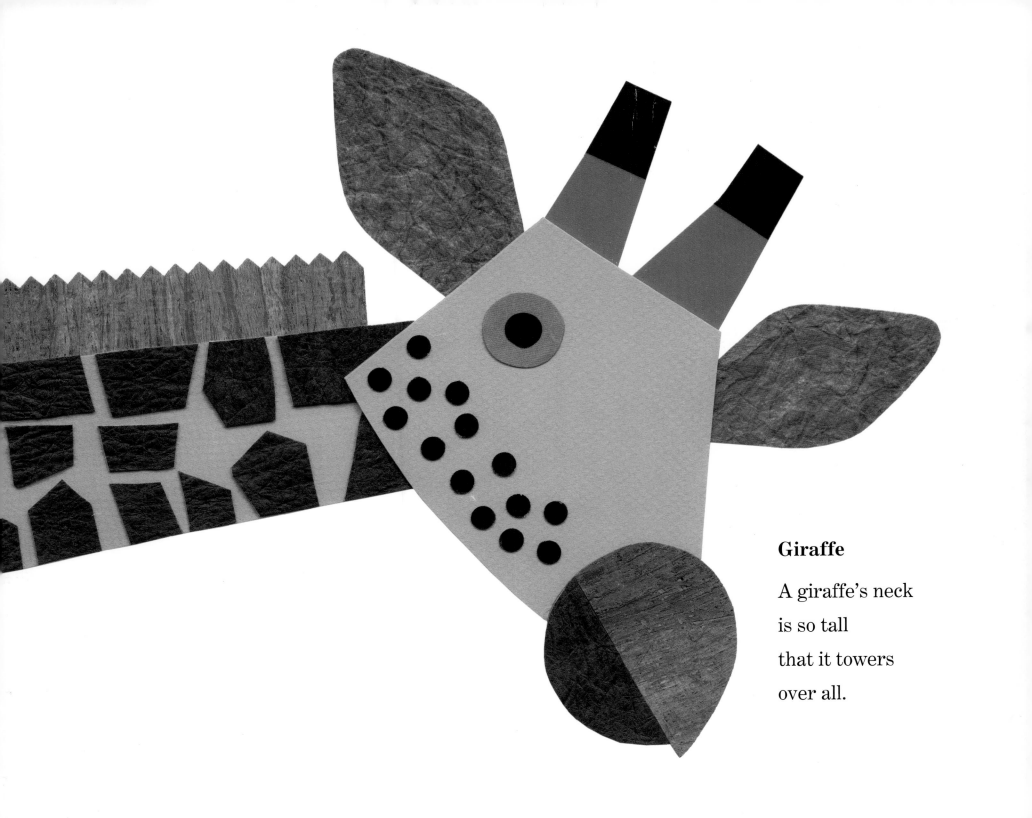

Giraffe

A giraffe's neck
is so tall
that it towers
over all.

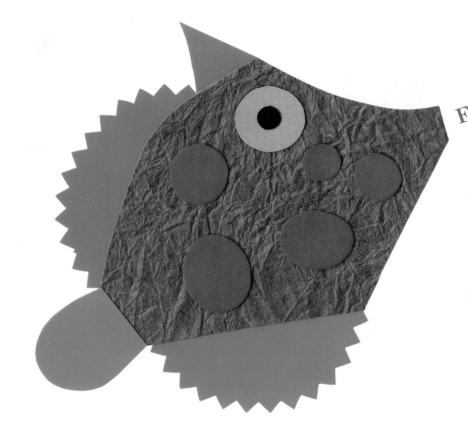

For Kailyn and Cali

BEACH LANE BOOKS
An imprint of Simon & Schuster Children's Publishing Division
1230 Avenue of the Americas, New York, New York 10020
Copyright © 2010 by Lois Ehlert
All rights reserved, including the right of reproduction in whole or in part in any form.
BEACH LANE BOOKS is a trademark of Simon & Schuster, Inc.
For information about special discounts for bulk purchases,
please contact Simon & Schuster Special Sales
at 1-866-506-1949 or business@simonandschuster.com.
The Simon & Schuster Speakers Bureau can bring authors to your live event.
For more information or to book an event,
contact the Simon & Schuster Speakers Bureau at 1-866-248-3049
or visit our website at www.simonspeakers.com.
The text for this book is set in Century Expanded.
The illustrations for this book are made of handmade and painted papers,
inks, and crayons.
Manufactured in China
1119 SCP
10 9 8 7
Library of Congress Cataloging-in-Publication Data
Ehlert, Lois.
Lots of spots / Lois Ehlert.—1st ed.
p. cm.
ISBN 978-1-4424-0289-8 (hardcover)
1. Camouflage (Biology)—Juvenile literature. I. Title.
QL759.E38 2010
591.472—dc22
2009034361

Animal Spots and Stripes

Animal appearances serve many functions. The ability to blend in with the natural surroundings through color or pattern can protect animals from predators. A gathering of zebras disrupts the shape of each individual animal and confuses a predator, as does a school of fish swimming together. Some chameleons can actually change colors to match their environment. Flounders and sand dabs can alter their body colors to blend with the ocean floor. I remember hiking in the woods and coming within two feet of a newborn white-tailed deer, hidden in the underbrush. It was so well camouflaged that I was unaware of its presence until someone pointed it out to me.

But some animals with stripes or spots don't hide: They want to be noticed. The white stripe of a skunk in the woods certainly gives a visual warning to detour or get sprayed. Many animals—such as the peacock with its spotted tail feathers—use color patterns to attract a mate. And some animals are just patterned beautifully—humans haven't yet figured out why.